Unguarded

Devilish #4

Charity Parkerson

Punk & Sissy Publications

Copyright

—Warning: This book is intended for readers over the age of 18. Some of my books contain allusions to past abuse and trauma.

Contents

Introduction

AN ACT OF BRAVERY landed Yuri in an odd but not unwelcome spot. Now his every day is spent with an alpha hellhound with an amazing tongue. He doesn't deserve it.

A lot of terrible acts and choices led Yuri into the path of a powerful godling. It's the best thing that's ever happened to him. He's found a family and a home. Maybe that home is in Hell, but beggars and all that. Now there's this rough and tumble hellhound who haunts his every waking moment, and Yuri doesn't know what to do. Brownie is an alpha. He's special. Everyone keeps saying Yuri is too, but he's not. He doesn't deserve this blessing.

Brownie is Lucifer's guardian hell-hound. He's top dog, even though Lucifer treats him like a pet. Not that Brownie is complaining. He has a good life, but he's always known that life was one he would travel alone. But now there's this wolf, and he's leagues above Brownie. It'll take a miracle for Yuri to see him as anything other than a friend. It's too bad they're both blind.

Unguarded is the fourth book in Charity Parkerson's Devilish series where vampires, Weres, demons, gods, and all manner of the supernatural live together beneath the noses of humankind.

These books are best when read in order.

Chapter One

IT SHOULDN'T MATTER, BUT it did. That was all Yuri could think as he paid for his own food and bought a new pair of jeans. He had never really had any human money of his own. As the son of an alpha, everything had been provided for him. Then the pack had torn his parents to pieces and Yuri had become a refugee in a new pack. At first, he had sung for his supper in a way. Talking shit was actually a forte of his that he didn't much use any longer. But when he had first come to town, he had used that skill to try to challenge the pack's alpha.

That hadn't worked for him. In fact, that had pretty much destroyed what was left of his life. Now Yuri was a pariah who lived in Hell, literally. Except today, everything felt weird and different. It shouldn't matter, but it did.

While Yuri hadn't made it to alpha, his overwhelming moronic behavior had somehow landed him in a higher position: guardian wolf to a godling. It was the highest position a wolf could achieve. In another odd twist of fate, that promotion and the change in location had given him a human bank account filled with the entire profit from the sale of a house in the mountains. The money should have gone to his godling, Riku. The house had actually been his, after all. Yet somehow fate kept handing Yuri all these blessings he didn't deserve, and Yuri felt like he held his breath all the time. Surely the other shoe would drop soon, and he would get his comeuppance, but no. He stood at the counter of the diner, inside a town of people who hated him, and paid for his own dinner. Yuri felt all the eyes upon him and the entire situation was eerie as hell. Reverence rolled from the pack rather than hatred, and really. It pissed him off because it shouldn't matter he was a guardian. He was the same wolf he had been before leaping into a fire to save Riku—who didn't even need to be saved, by the way. Yuri was the same wolf they had shunned even after he swallowed all the pride and submitted to their pack leader, Waylon. Now he outranked Waylon, and his family was a hodgepodge of a godling, the literal devil, and a sexy-ass hellhound he couldn't shake. The longer he waited to pay, the more the entire situation frayed his temper.

"Hey." The breathless-sounding greeting pulled Yuri from his growing black mood. A young wolf he had briefly met but couldn't recall slid between the counter and him, leaving less than a centimeter between their bodies.

"Kyrie," he said, reminding Yuri of his name.

Yuri nodded. "I remember." Of course, that was total bullshit.

Kyrie's yellow eyes flashed with interest as they slid down Yuri's body. Yuri wondered how the guy didn't draw the attention of the humans in town with those eyes. They were definitely unnatural. Maybe he told everyone he wore contacts. Sometimes Yuri's mind wandered off-topic. Kyrie still waited, as if he expected something. Yuri waited him out. He had nothing to say.

Kyrie broke first. Yuri had known he would since Yuri literally had nothing. "It's a full moon tonight."

"Okay." Really. What did he want Yuri to say? He knew it was a full moon. All wolves did. They couldn't resist the lunar pull.

That yellow stare slowly slid down Yuri's body again. Yuri fought the urge to shift uncomfortably. He was a guardian. Yuri had to stand tall and proud without fidgeting. Finally, Kyrie's gaze returned to holding his stare.

"Are you coming to tonight's full moon run?"

Oh. He was slow on the uptake, but not completely dumb. Yuri also wasn't interested, but he didn't want to hurt the guy's feelings. It wasn't Kyrie's fault. Until very recently, Yuri hadn't felt any attraction to anyone. He had always wondered if he was broken in some way. Honestly, he didn't have to wonder. He knew he was broken, but Brownie made him feel just a little less strange.

"Are you ready?"

There it was. Yuri fought the urge to close his eyes and lean back against the solid chest behind him. He felt the heat radiating from the huge hellhound at his back. The moment he had seen Brownie for the first time, he had come alive. In a single unguarded moment, he had never been more aware of every inch of his body. Brownie made everything about him sing.

Kyrie's gaze moved from Yuri to Brownie and back again. He didn't look worried. In fact, his eyebrows rose as if reminding Yuri he had asked a question.

Yuri cleared his throat and glanced over his shoulder. "I'm still waiting to pay."

"For fuck's sake." Brownie snatched the bill from Yuri's hand and stretched past them. His enormous body had no trouble sandwiching Yuri and Kyrie in against the counter. Brownie smacked the paper on the diner's counter and then dug a hundred-dollar bill from his wallet. He slapped that on top of the bill, catching the cook's attention. "This should cover things." His arm moved from the counter to Yuri's waist. He kept the zero space between them, making it impossible for Yuri to think clearly. "Let's go. This town gives me the creeps."

The claim pulled a laugh from Yuri. "Here? This place? You're from Hell. It's filled with demons and shit."

He let Brownie steer him to the door. Brownie had his full attention. Yuri didn't even watch where he walked. He simply let Brownie guide him while Kyrie was totally forgotten. Yuri was lost in Brownie's glowing red eyes. Now he was a beast who couldn't pass as a man, but goddamn. What a man he was in human form. Just muscle and scars and muscle. Fuck. Yuri ached. That full moon was really pulling at him. He had never wanted to lick every inch of someone in his entire life. Saliva filled his mouth at the thought of doing that to Brownie.

Brownie didn't release him—like he worried Yuri might see a squirrel and force him to stay ten minutes longer. A sexy slight smile played on Brownie's lips. "It's the people here," he said, pulling Yuri back on topic. "They're weird. In Hell, everyone is deceitful, but it's always on display. Here, they hide behind smiles. Like that kid back there. He wants to fuck you... or for you to fuck him." Brownie shrugged. "Either way, he should've just said that. Instead, he flirts with his eyes and hopes you'll notice."

Yuri's heart dropped. There it was. The thing that weighed on him every second of the day. While Brownie had brought Yuri's body all the way to life, Brownie didn't feel the same. As a hellhound alpha, he was probably leagues above Yuri. Yuri didn't really know how hierarchy worked in Hell. Not that it mattered. Brownie probably had loads of experience and found Yuri boring. Yuri got the feeling Brownie's life had been way more exciting than his. The only reason Brownie stayed glued to his side was because Lucifer ordered him to do so whenever he was outside Hell. Yuri was a huge prize for any deity who wanted to strike a blow at Lucifer. Since Riku was Lucifer's mate, and Riku was the only person Lucifer loved, it made sense. Hurting Yuri hurt Riku. So, here was

Brownie. Stuck with him: the boring wolf.

Brownie drew him to a stop. His gaze moved over Yuri's face. "You're upset."

Fuck. Sometimes he forgot they could read each other's minds. Some thoughts he needed to keep hidden. He scrambled for a lie that was close enough to the truth so Brownie wouldn't feel it was a lie. "I'm a wolf. This is a pack. I've never fit in, but I guess I sometimes want to."

Brownie's mind was on lockdown. Yuri couldn't see his thoughts. "You can go back to the kid, if you want."

Ouch. That one stung. "No."

Brownie gave him a sharp nod and started walking again.

Yuri wondered if the pains in his chest would kill him. He had lived in Hell for four months. Four months of sleeping across the hall from Brownie each night. One hundred and twenty nights of watching Brownie either go to bed without him or go out to wherever he partied with the hounds. He didn't invite Yuri. Yuri didn't fit anywhere. Sometimes, that hurt way more than he could handle. Today, it was heavy as hell.

Being with Yuri when he was in human form was a struggle. Yuri was flawless. The differences between them were on full display. Brownie was this beat-up, scarred hound from the depths. They didn't match. But he always found ways to touch Yuri because he couldn't fucking stop. Anytime Yuri let him, he groomed him. Goddess, he tasted like ambrosia. He was the closest to heaven Brownie would ever be. Brownie needed to head to the bar and find someone to fuck. He shouldn't be here, sitting in the corner and watching Yuri pace.

From the moment they returned to Hell, Yuri had been in wolf form, walking the floor like the trapped animal he was. He had Brownie's stomach in knots. That young wolf who had been flirting with Yuri earlier was beautiful. He matched Yuri. Was he the reason Yuri paced? Did he want to go enjoy his world with someone who actually matched him? Brownie was scared as hell of his thoughts. Was Yuri angry Brownie had pulled him away from his friend?

"Okay. Spill. What in the fuck is wrong with you? All your pacing has the hair on the back of my neck irritated."

Yuri immediately stopped and sat at Riku's barked question.

Lucifer stroked Riku's thigh. They were practically molded as one, reading a book together. "It's a full moon tonight."

At Lucifer's words, a hint of relief washed over Brownie. Yuri wasn't upset with him. He was just restless.

"You should join the full moon run."

I was invited.

Brownie felt sick at Yuri's mental response.

"Then go."

I'm not one of them. Yuri went back to pacing. His dark mood crushed Brownie's chest.

"So do it here."

Yuri stopped pacing at Lucifer's suggestion.

Am I allowed to do that?

He just said you could. He's the boss. Even as Brownie reassured Yuri, he double-checked with Lucifer. "Will he be safe?"

"No demon would dare cross me by touching him. You should go too. The two of you are killing our vibe. Maybe we want to get messy."

Ew.

Brownie laughed at Yuri's reaction. His mood was fully restored at the thought of taking Yuri for a run. The woods in Hell might be on fire, but they still smelled like freedom. It was still space to hit full speed and let out all the wolf's energy. He could show Yuri how he could be just as happy here.

Brownie jumped to his feet and headed for the door. His deadly claws clicked on the floor with every step. *Why do you always 'ew' at them? They're mates and sex is awesome.*

If you say so.

Brownie froze. He couldn't help it. One foot was out the front door and his entire body came to a halt. *Do you not think so?* Because that was strange as hell for an animal.

Wow. I know I'm weird, but you didn't have to say it.

You weren't meant to hear that thought.

Yuri rolled his eyes and pushed past him before slipping out the door.

Brownie was hot on his heels. *Seriously. You don't like sex?*

I thought we were running.

Why are you so uncomfortable? Brownie had no idea why he was being so pushy and defensive—like Yuri's feelings were a personal affront. He had just never wanted to fuck someone so badly in his life, and Yuri didn't enjoy sex. What the fuck?

I didn't say I don't like sex. You assumed that's what I meant. Unless this conversation is leading to you actually fucking me, then tag. You're it. He bumped Brownie with his head and took off like a shot.

Brownie stood frozen for half a second. Had that been an invitation? What did he even mean? Fuck. Yuri ran through a forest filled with demons, hounds, and countless other monsters. He had to move his ass. Brownie shot out after Yuri. He heard Yuri's laughter ringing through his mind—like music to his soul. Brownie found himself holding back, toying with Yuri. Hellhounds were five times faster than wolves. They were built to chase down souls on the run. Nothing could outpace them. He could easily overtake Yuri, but he wanted Yuri to run off some energy. Unfortunately, the alpha hunter in him had been unleashed. The needs the full moon awoke in Yuri affected him every second he stayed in Yuri's head. Maybe Yuri didn't naturally crave sex the way his wolf buddies did when the lunar cycle hit this stage, but Brownie felt it by proxy.

Nan nanny boo boo. You can't catch me.

A very animalistic smile stretched his mouth, baring his deadly teeth at Yuri's childish taunt. *Think you've got a chance? What'll you give me if I do?* Brownie didn't wait for Yuri to answer. He leapt, paws striking the nearest tree. He used the momentum to get as much height as possible before tackling Yuri from above. Brownie pulled his weight so he wouldn't hurt Yuri, but he ensured he couldn't get away either.

Yuri turned human as he hit the ground. Peals of loud laughter cut through the otherwise haunting woods. He rolled beneath Brownie. His bright smile was the most beautiful thing Brownie had ever seen. They were both fully aroused. Brownie was too close to the animal side tonight to control himself. He turned human and lowered his weight, ensuring Yuri understood he was hard for him, and he was in danger.

"Caught you." Even he heard the demonic edge to his tone. He was the hellhound alpha now. No turning back. This side took what it wanted.

Yuri's chest heaved from the exertion. His smile didn't dim even after Brownie made it clear he was ready to rip into that tight asshole of his. "What did we decide was your prize again? I don't remember."

If Brownie wasn't in full alpha mode, he wouldn't have answered. He was too far gone to think about who was beneath him. "A kiss."

The happiness swimming in Yuri's eyes didn't dim. "I don't remember agreeing to that, but okay."

Reality struck, hitting him like a truck. It was Yuri. Yuri was beneath him, hard, and agreeing to let Brownie kiss him. He didn't know what to do. Hellhounds didn't kiss. He didn't even know why he had suggested it. He had never wanted a kiss before. Brownie knew it had been his idea, but hellhounds weren't gentle. They came together violently. It wasn't like they could trust each other not to rip out the other's throat. Brownie just thought about Yuri's lips more than he understood. He was frozen.

Brownie didn't have to decide how to proceed. Yuri lifted his head and gave Brownie the kiss he had won. Brownie jerked back. He didn't know if he liked the way that felt—like he could lose himself. Then he watched Yuri turn skittish. He felt the way he withdrew. His chest hurt. He didn't think. Brownie just lowered his head and touched his mouth to Yuri's. He had no idea what he was doing.

Yuri's tongue slid across his bottom lip before his teeth lightly sank into it. He tugged. Brownie was transfixed by every sensation. Butterflies fluttered in his gut. His skin tingled. Brownie's brain itched. His lips automatically parted. Yuri's tongue slipped inside his mouth and curled around Brownie's tongue. A soft moan escaped him without his permission. He already pictured Yuri doing that to his dick. The idea equally pissed him off because his Yuri kneeled for no one. Damn. He really hadn't realized how sexy and vulnerable he would feel with Yuri's tongue in his mouth.

"That does look yummy. Care to share?"

Brownie was full hellhound again in an instant, keeping Yuri protected beneath his enormous, solid body. "He's mine." He kept his gaze leveled on the red-eyed demon that stood, ready to pounce. It was a lust demon. One touch to Yuri's skin and he would be addicted.

"What's the fun in that? Two is always better than one."

Turn wolf and run. Don't look back. Go home. No detours.

Proving he was a smart wolf, Yuri immediately did as told. Brownie only shifted his weight enough for Yuri to run free. Otherwise, he stayed planted and ready for anything.

The demon's eyes followed Yuri. "Awww. It's a sweet puppy." His gaze moved back to Brownie. An evil-looking smile stretched his lips. "I have his scent now. I can wait."

Fuck, Yuri definitely wouldn't be allowed to leave the castle unguarded again now. Brownie knew he could declare Yuri's position to Lucifer's mate. That would only protect Yuri for now. It would do more damage in the future when word spread. No one knew Lucifer's business. He couldn't reveal any weak spots.

"Move along. You're on Lucifer's land."

"Everything is Lucifer's land, but I know you're doing your job."

Yuri says there's a problem. Show me what you see.

Brownie could handle one stray demon, but Lucifer was his master. He obeyed.

Oh. It's Jetaime. He's harmless.

It was obvious Jetaime saw Lucifer in his eyes. He took a step back. "The scent of lust called to me. Hunger won. Have a good night, beast." Jetaime wandered away.

Brownie watched until he no longer had any scent of the guy. Only then did he head back home. He walked slower than necessary. His head was all over the place. Like a coward, he slipped inside through the dungeons and made his way through back channels to get to his bedroom. Brownie couldn't see Yuri again tonight. That kiss had him fucked up.

Chapter Two

YURI SPENT HOURS PACING his bedroom floor. He kept the door open so he could see Brownie's door. Yuri didn't want to miss him. Worry ate him alive. He was too young to always feel this sick, but life never took it easy on him. He walked until his paws ached and he passed out in the middle of the floor. Yuri woke tucked perfectly in his bed and no memory of how he had gotten there, but Brownie's scent lingered in the room.

He rolled and stared at the wall. The way Brownie had looked at him when Yuri kissed him wouldn't leave his head. The poor guy had been horrified, but then he had come back for more. How far would things have gone if they hadn't been interrupted? He had a bad feeling he would never find out. Yuri swore he felt Brownie missing from him. He rubbed his chest. Sometimes, when he focused really hard, he swore he felt Brownie in his head. It was comforting, knowing Brownie could feel what he did. Brownie was an alpha. Of course he could read Yuri. Yuri had alpha blood too. Maybe he just needed to hone it a little better. It was equally possible he needed to stop depending so much on Brownie. In his heart, he knew they would never happen. He just wasn't enough or something. It had been that way his entire life. He had to get out of here. Being this close to what he could never have all the time was breaking him.

Yuri climbed from the bed and headed for the bathroom. He went through his entire morning routine while avoiding his reflection. Apparently, there was nothing to see. A deep self-hatred had settled into his soul. He had to escape. He dressed in his new outfit, hoping anything at all would help his mental health. Nothing worked. He headed for the sitting room while praying he didn't run across anyone along the way. Riku was on the couch, reading. He barely glanced up as Yuri strolled through the room.

"I'm going to visit Frost."

Riku flashed him a smile. "Okay. Is Brownie not going with you?"

Yuri ground his back teeth for a second before responding. "Haven't seen him, but I survived all on my own before I met any of you. I'll be fine."

Riku held his stare. His expression stayed blank. "Do you want to talk about it?"

He couldn't. Everything felt wrong. He had to be free. "No."

Riku stood. "Come on. I'll give you a leg up."

The only way out of Hell—at least for him—was through a mirror above Riku and Lucifer's bed. It was a bit of a leap for most creatures. Riku, being a godling, had no trouble helping Yuri make the climb.

Yuri poked his head through the mirror first, making sure he didn't disturb anyone. The mirror led to a room inside Frost's house. Since he was the town of Wulfe's healer, sometimes he needed to be reached quickly. The mirror was a huge intrusion into the man's home. So they had set up the mirror in a room where no one could walk directly into their home—thanks to binding spells. However, they could walk out the back door, circle the cabin past a slew of vampire guards, and knock on the front door. It was the best compromise for everyone.

Frost allowed Yuri to keep a backpack near the back door so he could be ready to change forms easily and keep clothes with him. Yuri snagged it on his way out in case he chose to stay in the woods tonight.

With the sun still shining brightly, the vamps were all at half strength. That still made them stronger than any wolf. He nodded at familiar faces as he passed, but he didn't try to make conversation. Yuri wasn't fit for company. He needed to reclaim his independence. That plan lasted less time than expected.

A red-haired vampire named Fen was headed for a pickup truck as Yuri rounded the cabin. He flashed Yuri a smile. "Are you headed into town?"

Yuri forced his shit mood to the back burner. Fen had been kidnapped by an angry god because of Lucifer and Riku. He had been returned by the king of the Americas shortly after. Despite him seeming no worse for the wear, Yuri still felt oddly guilty for the inconvenience.

"Yeah. I hoped to hit the diner before I make my way up the mountain."

Fen motioned toward the truck. "Hop in. I'll give you a lift."

Since Fen had to travel the human way during the daylight hours, Yuri might as well keep him company. Plus, the quicker he got started up the mountain and away from Brownie, the better. "Thanks. I appreciate it."

"No problem."

They didn't speak again until they were on the road. "I think this is the first time I've seen you without Lucifer's hound in ages."

Fuck. His chest hurt. "Yeah. I think he's busy torturing the damned with Lucifer today. Plus, I just need a break from all things Hell related. The fresh air and wilderness are calling to me today."

Fen nodded but kept his gaze locked on the road. "I can't even imagine. It must be hard being cooped up all the time. I've nae personally been to Hell, but I've heard stories. It does nae sound fun."

Even though Fen wasn't looking at him, Yuri shrugged. "Sometimes. I mean, anything I want is mine with the snap of Riku's fingers, but it's still Hell. It's still not safe for me to run through the woods. There are no full moons or sunny days." Funny how he hadn't noticed the loss until Brownie kissed him and then hid from him like Yuri was a mistake. It was cool. He didn't need anyone. "What about you, though? How have you been? I feel bad I haven't checked on you. Are you good since you got dragged into the gods' bullshit?"

Fen flashed him a smile. "It's all good. I'm guessing Celeste wiped the memories from me. If nae for everyone else worrying over me, I nae might have known anything happened at all."

He was glad to hear that. Fen hadn't deserved any of this. "So, no problems at all? That's great."

Fen shrugged. "I'll admit I've been starved ever since then. It's slightly maddening. It's like no blood is good enough or food satisfies me. Like nothing tastes good any longer. I haven't experienced that since I was first turned."

Yuri was officially distracted from his bullshit. "You were once human?"

Fen nodded. "I was a warrior and was cut down on the battlefield. If a vampire hadn't turned me, I would nae have survived."

"Huh. I guess I never really think about people being turned. All Weres are born or are human mates. It must have been a heck of a transition."

Fen's hand lifted from the steering wheel and dropped again in a dismissive motion. "It was a long time ago. I remember verra little about those days."

The diner came into sight. He suddenly wasn't as confident about eating alone. "Would you like to eat with me? My treat."

Fen found a parking spot. "Maybe some ice cream or something. I'm still trying my ass off to find something I can tolerate."

Together, they climbed from the truck and headed inside. It was still slightly early for dinner. There were plenty of tables open. They chose one and sat. Yuri wasn't finding comfort in silence today. He had to keep the conversation alive.

"Have you tried getting blood from only humans since your return? Maybe you're drained in a way that requires something more powerful."

Fen looked thoughtful for a moment. His green eyes caught the light in an unnatural way that held Yuri's attention. He was a handsome guy. Fen looked like the Scottish warrior he was. "That's a fair point," Fen said finally. "Vampires don't bite each other often for fear of accidentally ending up mated to someone who isn't their fated mate, so yeah. I've stuck to humans."

"Wait. Vampires can end up mated to someone not fated for them?" Yuri was woefully ignorant of the vampire world. His pack hadn't welcomed them.

Fen's eyes swam with laughter. "It's nae verra common. Like I said, we avoid taking each other's blood if we can, but yeah. If things got heated and a blood exchange occurred, then they would be bonded and stuck until one or the other died. Which obviously doesn't happen often, of course. So you could really fuck up an eternity if you're nae careful."

"Fascinating." Really. It was. He wished he had spent more time getting to know other species. Sometimes he felt out of his depth. He spent a ton of time with Brownie, but he still knew next to nothing about hellhounds. Yuri wanted to learn more about their world. It was much bigger than his father had ever wanted him to discover. Keep him isolated. Keep him ignorant. Teach Yuri to be a monster just like him. Yuri wasn't him.

Yuri waited until they ordered to ask any more questions. The only way to leave his past behind was to learn everything he could about as many be-ings as he could. "What about Weres? Surely we have stronger blood than a human. That might be a place to start."

Fen laughed. "Are you volunteering?"

He didn't think Fen meant for him to take the question seriously, but he did. Yuri gave it some real thought for half a second. "Well, I mean, I'm a guardian wolf to a godling. Maybe that means nothing, or maybe it's something. I don't really know, but people keep telling me that's as high as any wolf can climb. Not that I know if that actually affects the strength of my blood. I'm very much a backwoods wolf from a secretive pack. We didn't welcome outsiders, and we weren't taught our hierarchy. I imagine my dad kept it that way for a reason. If there was no one higher, then he would always be seen as the top dog." A terrible one. The one that got him killed. Yuri had rambled too much. He got to the point. "So, yeah. I guess if you're willing, then I am."

Their ice cream came.

Fen never looked away from Yuri. It was as if he tried to solve a puzzle. When they were alone again, Fen gave him a sharp nod. He picked up the salt-shaker and salted his ice cream.

A laugh burst from Yuri at the move. "Really? Salt on ice cream."

A smile snapped to Fen's lips. "I told you everything has tasted terrible. Another vampire I know—who is a fairly recent turn—eats this all the time. I'm willing to give anything a shot."

Yuri shook his head. "Why didn't you try it on a spoonful first? You might not like it."

A bark of laughter burst from Fen. "I didn't really think about that." He took a bite and curled his nose.

Yuri pushed Fen's bowl aside and moved his to the center of the table. "We can share."

Fen shook his head. "It's okay. Since you offered your blood, I'll wait for that if you're not offended."

He practically felt Fen's hunger and agitation rolling off his skin. Yuri waved their server over. "Would it be okay if I get everything to go?" He had ordered a rare hamburger for after their ice cream, but he wouldn't make Fen suffer.

"You don't have to do that. I can wait."

Yuri shrugged. "It's fine. I'm not much good for anything else, but I can do this."

Fen was back to staring at him like he couldn't figure him out. "I should probably warn you that getting bitten can cause a sexual response. In humans, I block their minds. They don't know anything happened. Considering your position as a guardian wolf, I don't think I can block you."

Had that been what Fen had been doing with the intense staring? Had he tried to control Yuri's mind just to see if he could? Not that it mattered, he guessed. He had already agreed to do this. Yuri took a bite of his ice cream, scraping the bowl. He was a little surprised how fast he had eaten. He kept his gaze locked on his task. "Don't worry about me. I'm pretty sure I'm broken in that department. No one interests me." He felt the claim as the blatant lie it was. There was one person who made Yuri want everything.

Fen didn't embarrass him or treat him like he was broken. In fact, he did the opposite. "Ah. You have a living un-claimed mate somewhere. I've heard of people losing interest in everyone once they near the time to meet their other half. In theory, it's supposed to help you spot your mate when you meet them. No one else will do."

Yuri smiled. He only had interest in Brownie, and that was impossible. "That's a nice theory, and I appreciate you trying to make me feel better. But I've been like this my entire life. So I'm not so sure that's the reason I am the way I am. It's okay, though. I've always been a bit of a loner wolf."

The box of food appeared in front of him. Yuri motioned for the woman to wait as he dug out his wallet. He passed her enough money to cover the meal and tip. When she walked away, he grabbed his box and focused on Fen. "Are you ready?"

They stood and headed out. Darkness had begun to tint the sky, turning it a mixture of purple and orange.

Yuri motioned for Fen to follow him to the back of the building. "I'm about to slip into the woods back here and head up the mountain, if you'd like to do this now."

Fen touched his shoulder and pulled him to a stop. When Yuri turned, Fen immediately moved into his space. "Best we do this quickly before you think too much about it."

Before Yuri had a chance to even wonder what to expect, Fen's mouth was on his neck. He felt the first pull of blood from his veins. Fen moaned against his skin. Yuri wanted to claim he didn't respond, but he did. It seemed he wasn't strong enough to avoid the effects after all. Still, he stood rigid. He wouldn't make this uncomfortable for Fen. The guy was starving. This wasn't personal. As always, he couldn't form the illusion of anyone being interested in him. This was just Yuri buying the guy dinner. He fought a slightly hysterical laugh at the thought. Then Fen pulled away. His eyes were closed, and he looked like a man who had just gotten fucked.

When Fen's eyes opened, they glowed an even brighter green. "Thank you." He sounded breathless. "You have extremely powerful blood. That helped quite a bit."

A smile snapped to Yuri's lips. He hadn't been useless for once. "You're welcome."

"You're not useless, even without having fed me. Blood this powerful doesn't happen to everyone. It's earned. You're special, whether you see it or not."

Fen really was a nice guy. He hoped everything worked out for him. "Thank you for that." He glanced toward the trees. The wilderness called for him.

Fen took a step back. "Go. I feel the restlessness in your wolf."

Yuri smiled. "I'll see you again soon."

Fen gave him a sharp nod and walked away. Yuri watched him go. He genuinely hoped he had helped Fen for real. That it hadn't just been talk on Fen's part. There was nothing special about Yuri. Everyone knew it.

At the edge of nightfall, a wave of tremendous fury slammed into Brownie. It was so hard and fast, Brownie had immediately gone in search of Yuri. They were connected in some way and something had happened. Brownie just didn't know what. It felt almost like jealousy—like Yuri had chosen someone else. He knew that day would come sometime, but he wasn't ready. Brownie wanted to tear someone to shreds. It was unreasonable and didn't even make sense. Considering the way Yuri had paced the floor all night until he dropped, his sweet wolf probably still slept soundly in the bed where Brownie had placed him. Yuri's bedroom door was open. His bed was empty. Even Yuri's scent barely lingered any longer.

The sound of Brownie's combat boots hitting the floor with every angry step reverberated from the marble walls. He heard Yuri's name as he neared the sitting room. His feet froze. He would like to claim he wasn't one to eavesdrop, but he was. In fact, he was a hell of a spy. Brownie held his breath and strained his superior hearing.

"I'm just worried about my wolf."

"He'll be fine." Lucifer didn't sound bored by the conversation exactly. It was more like they'd had this discussion a million times.

"I really think it's time to say something. You didn't see his face. It was almost like he hated me—like I'm keeping him from freedom. He doesn't understand why he feels the way he does. This isn't fair to him."

Lucifer sighed. "Come here." A moment passed before Lucifer spoke again. "Do you really want to say something and then watch him choose this life out of obligation?"

"That's not how it feels and you know it."

Lucifer's voice muffled, as if he spoke against Riku's skin. "In this case, I very much fear that's exactly how it feels.

You've seen and heard all the same things as I have. Some things can't be rushed."

Brownie didn't understand. Did they worry Yuri only stayed here out of a sense of duty? Yuri loved Riku. That was why he stayed. And if they were freely speaking of him, where in the fuck was he? He wasn't in his room. Yuri wasn't with them. Brownie closed his eyes and focused. His mind hunted the familiar sensation of Yuri's soul. As a hellhound, he had the unique ability to find any soul anywhere. If they had a jail break, his kind would be sent to retrieve the damned. Yuri's soul was particularly bright. Maybe that was why Brownie was such a moth to his flame.

Behind closed lids, he swore he smelled the fresh grass. He felt the wind on his skin. A vision of tall weeds swaying against the edge of the night sky filled his mind. The wind blowing the tall blades from side to side was almost hypnotic. A sense of euphoria overcame him—like he had been drugged or... had lost a lot of blood. That was a feeling he knew too well.

Brownie's eyes shot open. Yuri was in trouble. He was obviously in a field on his stomach somewhere, catching glimpses of the stars while goddess knew what happened to him. Had he been attacked? Did he lie there waiting to be found and rescued? He didn't understand.

Brownie marched through the living room, heading straight for Lucifer's bedroom. "I'm going to get Yuri."

Riku and Lucifer barely looked his way from their spot, cuddled on the couch. "Okay."

Honestly, he found their lack of argument a bit strange but he didn't turn down a gift. He was scared for anyone who tried stopping him right now. Brownie easily leapt through the mirror, landing inside Frost's home. His gaze immediately shot to where Yuri's backpack stayed. It was gone. The air left his lungs in a whoosh. There was a real chance Yuri might have decided to move along. He still didn't know what Lucifer and Riku had been talking about. Yuri really might have decided to leave him. He needed to apologize about last night. Even if Yuri chose not to return, he needed to at least beg Yuri not to hate him for that kiss. He shouldn't have attacked the guy like that. Yuri was a wolf of honor. Brownie had a duty to ensure that Yuri be respected at all times. He was fucking furious with himself and all the desires he couldn't control. Brownie was better than that, though. He would make this right.

Brownie stepped outside into the night air. Before he could close his eyes and follow his senses, his head whipped toward the vampire standing guard outside the door. He didn't think. Brownie pounced, taking the vampire to the ground. He felt the way the guy tried to move through time and space to escape Brownie's hold, but there was no escaping a hellhound. No creature but Lucifer was above him. Everyone had the possibility of ending up in Hell. That meant he had been given the ability to overpower any beast.

Confusion crossed the vamp's features. More vampires appeared, shouting as they attempted to pry Brownie from his prey. He barely noticed their efforts.

"You smell like his blood." He lowered his head and inhaled, trying to determine if it was internal or external. Fuck. The scent pumped through his veins. "You drank his blood." The growl that coated each word should have terrified the man beneath him.

Instead, he looked slightly amused. "Oh. There you are."

He had no idea what that meant. "You have two seconds to tell me if that blood was freely given."

Unexpectedly, a vision filled his head. The vamp's fangs were buried in Yuri's vein, his mouth on Yuri's neck. He felt Yuri's indifference to the bite. Yuri merely felt like he did a favor for a friend.

Brownie pushed to his feet and towed the vampire up along with him. "I had to check."

"What in the fuck are you doing?" The yelled question finally penetrated his focus on the vampire with Yuri's blood. He glanced over his shoulder at the irate vampire and then chose to ignore him. "Your friend is more upset than you are. You should look into that..." One eyebrow lifted as it occurred to him he didn't even know the guy's name.

"Fen. My friend is a warrior. It's in his blood to protect. Nae worry about me. I might've reacted the same if I smelled my mate's blood on another man. Not that I have a mate."

Brownie blinked, and then blinked again. He thought to say Yuri wasn't his mate, but the words refused to cross his lips.

The laughter swimming in Fen's eyes deepened. "Oh."

He kept saying that while silently laughing at Brownie. It was kind of pissing him off. Luckily for Fen, he bowed out of the conversation.

"I wasn't aware you didn't know. That's a little awkward for me. You should go find Yuri. He said the wilderness called to him and headed up the mountain."

Brownie dipped his chin. He refused to admit or deny anything. When he was out from beneath their stares and the threat of a horde of vamps, he would mull over his predicament. "Thank you. I'll have no trouble tracking him." He didn't wait to chat. Brownie ran for the woods. He was every bit as fast in human form as he was in hound mode. Still, he didn't move as quickly as he could. Mate? Fen's words kept bouncing off the walls of his brain. It couldn't be true. As a guardian wolf, Yuri likely outranked him. That thought froze Brownie's feet to the ground. That title absolutely ranked Yuri above him.

He shouldn't be able to hear Yuri's thoughts. Brownie was so used to being the top dog, which gave him the ability to penetrate the mind of any lesser beings, it never occurred to him to question why he could hear Yuri. But Yuri wasn't a lesser. Even if being guardian put him on the same level as Brownie, he would need Yuri's permission to hear his thoughts. From their very first encounter, they had spoken mentally.

Brownie bent at the waist and sucked air. It wasn't enough. He went down on his haunches. Holy shit. Yuri was his mate. Not only was Yuri his mate, Lucifer and Riku knew it. That was what they had discussed. Riku had wanted to tell them. Lucifer had not, for fear Brownie would feel duty-bound to claim Yuri. He wasn't wrong. The sense of responsibility overwhelmed him to the point of bringing him to his knees. His mate was out there, unclaimed. Celeste had told him he would be blessed beyond his wildest dreams. He hadn't known. This was so much bigger than he dared to dream. Holy fuck. He had to get to his mate. His mate. Brownie sat. His ass simply hit the ground without his consent. He had a mate... the most beautiful mate he had ever seen. Did Yuri know? Had he felt rejected last night? Was that why he left? Brownie couldn't breathe. For once, he didn't know where to go from here.

Chapter Three

FROM HIS SPOT ON his stomach in the tall grass, and with his eyes turned up toward the moon, the sky swayed between the weeds. He felt slightly high from Fen taking his blood. It was possible Fen had taken too much without either of them noticing. It was kind of nice, though. He felt like he floated on a cloud. Maybe Yuri should take up drinking. Of course, he would likely burn through the alcohol too quickly to enjoy it. This, too, would pass faster than any human could endure. For now, he enjoyed thinking about anything other than Brownie.

Brownie. Sigh. Yuri rolled onto his back and let the moonlight shine on his stomach. The beams were like vitamin D for his wolfy soul. That was something only a Were would understand. He felt Brownie before the guy's heat enveloped him. Yuri turned human as Brownie's body covered his. Brownie was in full leather. Yuri was a little ashamed of how hot that look made him.

"You're so very sexy." Whoa. Had he said that out loud? He felt a little light-headed. Yuri needed to bite his tongue.

"Wow. You really are my mate. No one in the history of ever has said that to me."

Yuri blinked. Mate? Was he hallucinating? "What do you mean?"

A sexy, wicked smile stretched Brownie's lips. "At least I'm not the only one who didn't know."

"Wait." Yuri was confused. "Are you serious? But... what? I'm not complaining. It's just... are you sure? I can't imagine Celeste would bless me like that. I don't deserve it."

"Let's find out." Brownie took Yuri's arm and bit.

Yuri hadn't been prepared. Not by a long shot. His entire back bowed. A loud gasp tore from his lips. His body jerked. An orgasm tore through him. He shook from the power of it. He might have been humiliated by the way he blew all over Brownie's sexy leather, except Brownie stared at the place he had bitten with shock etching his features. Yuri imagined he looked the same. There it was—a scar proving he belonged to Brownie. Their gazes met. Yuri made it half a second. Brownie had to belong to him too. He snagged Brownie's head and hauled him down. Yuri didn't hesitate. His teeth tore into Brownie's neck above his collar. Scalding blood filled his mouth. Yuri swallowed. The tug of being stitched together was undeniable. Brownie made noises that had Yuri wanting to pat himself on the back. He pulled away. Yuri had to watch the wound turn to his mark. Brownie was his.

An amazing rough tongue filled his mouth. Yuri lost the ability to focus on anything other than his mate's kiss. His mate. Wow. He was moved beyond words. Brownie was everything he wanted for himself. The only thing he wanted. His entire life had been driven by desperation and pain. He spent so much time hiding behind various personalities, he wasn't sure who he was anymore, but he knew he was always unhappy. Yuri hadn't been since the first time he spoke to Brownie. He couldn't believe this amazing thing had happened.

"I think we've officially ruined this outfit."

Yuri laughed against Brownie's lips. "I'll buy you a new one."

He loved the sound of Brownie's laughter. It was deep and made goosebumps rise on Yuri's skin. Brownie buried his face against Yuri's throat and inhaled. Yuri savored every sensation.

Brownie licked. "Goddess, I love grooming you. You taste like how I imagine heaven does." He licked again.

Yuri felt every taste bud slide across his skin. Just like the first night Brownie had dragged his tongue through Yuri's fur, Yuri couldn't focus on anything else.

"I would've chosen you."

Warmth spread through Yuri's chest at Brownie's whispered confession.

"Even if Celeste hadn't given you to me, I still would've picked you above any other creature. The first time I set eyes on you, I was yours."

Yuri's throat swelled. His eyes burned. No one had ever made him feel the way Brownie did—like he was special. He wasn't. "I don't know what I did to deserve you, but I'm so fucking grateful. You have no idea." Or maybe he did. Brownie could see his thoughts. They were always in each other's heads. A watery-sounding chuckle escaped Yuri. "How did we not notice?"

Brownie held Yuri tighter. "I'm used to hearing everyone's thoughts, and I never dreamed you'd want me. Even being my mate, I didn't know if you'd want me."

He couldn't believe such a sexy, confident, and hardened creature would think he wasn't worthy of anything. It was true, though. Yuri saw it in his mind. He had genuinely believed Yuri was out of his reach.

Yuri didn't know how much he could forcibly share mentally, but he tried. He rested his temple against Brownie's and showed him all the times he had longed. Yuri let him see how Brownie looked in his eyes. His strength called to Yuri, because way too many times in his life, he had been too weak to protect himself. He loved the way he felt with Brownie—safe. Protected. Cherished.

"You are all those things." Brownie's lips skimmed the shell of Yuri's ear. His hot breath against Yuri's skin had goosebumps skirting down Yuri's body. Yuri was on fire, like Brownie hadn't just made him blow. "Fuck." The whispered curse against his ear made Yuri pant. "You make me want to do things I never have before. I don't kiss." His lips trailed down Yuri's neck. "That's all I want to do when I'm with you. My lips ache to touch you."

Yuri was completely his. There was nothing Brownie could do Yuri would refuse. He wanted everything. His fingers dug into Brownie's muscular arms. He wanted to hold on to the moment forever.

"You have no idea how badly I want to make love to you, but I know you don't like that."

Yuri's brain stuttered for a second. "Wait. What?"

Brownie kissed his collarbone, moving lower. "You said you don't like sex."

"Again, I didn't say that. You assumed that's what I meant."

Brownie pulled away and met Yuri's stare. "Then what did you mean when you implied sex wasn't awesome."

He shouldn't be embarrassed. This was his mate. Yuri just hated feeling exposed. He shrugged. Even he felt how uncomfortable the gesture appeared. His gaze slid away. It was suddenly a lot harder to look into the eyes that haunted him. "I guess it's more like I wouldn't know."

He felt the way Brownie intentionally kept his thoughts blank. "You're a virgin."

"I didn't say that either. Being the alpha's son didn't spare me." Fuck. He hated saying that and if Brownie wanted more from him, he wouldn't get it. The pack had torn his father apart for a reason. He'd had a sickness. If anything, Yuri was even more convenient than any other child had been.

Brownie's lips returned to Yuri's neck, wiping away the past. Only the way he felt beneath Brownie existed now. He made Yuri want to be touched... only by him. A deadly-sounding growl vibrated against Yuri's neck. The sound went straight to Yuri's cock like a caress.

"Damn right I'll be the only one touching you."

A sad smile pulled at Yuri's lips. He had a hard time holding on to it. Brownie had nothing to worry about. Yuri had less than zero interest in being with anyone else. But he knew he would never have the same loyalty, and that hurt. Brownie was an alpha. He wouldn't be faithful. It was expected of him to grow the pack.

Brownie sat back on his heels and stared down at Yuri with a closed expression. It was like he was angry and trying to hide it. After a second, he snagged Yuri's backpack and dragged it closer. He pulled out a t-shirt and cleaned their skin the best he could before pulling out the blanket Yuri kept stuffed in the bag for cold nights. With his thoughts kept on lockdown from Yuri, Brownie wrapped Yuri in the blanket. His gaze avoided Yuri's. Yuri had a bad feeling Brownie didn't want Yuri to see his rage, but Yuri didn't know what he had done wrong. This was a familiar feeling, though. He was always the fuck-up. Everyone shut him out.

Brownie's gaze shot to his, as if he heard that thought. "You're mine. I've told you a dozen times hellhounds aren't wolves. Our world isn't like yours. The only way hellhounds are created is by Lucifer's hand. Nothing is expected of me but to guard him... and now to be your mate. I'm not a wolf," he repeated, sounding angry. He stood and plucked Yuri's tightly wrapped body from the ground. In a flash, Yuri found himself over Brownie's massive shoulder. He ground his back teeth, trying not to think and piss off Brownie more than he obviously had. Brownie slung Yuri's backpack over his other shoulder and took off like a shot. Oddly, Yuri didn't feel the least bit unsecured. He didn't get beaten to death by a bumpy ride. Brownie kept him tucked tightly in a way that simply had Yuri along for his run. But his position made it hard to keep up with where they were. He sort of recognized the floor of Frost's house before a leap through the mirror had him staring at Lucifer's bed. That disappeared just as quickly as Brownie strode through the castle at a clipped pace. If they passed Lucifer or Riku, Yuri didn't see them or hear them. The air left his lungs as he landed on a soft mattress. Everything smelled like Brownie. Yuri wanted to roll around in the scent and keep it for later. But his gaze refused to budge from Brownie long enough for him to do anything. Brownie stripped. He was so fucking sexy. The scar, showing him as Yuri's mate, caught and held his attention. It nearly blended with a ragged scar Brownie already had. That thought led to another. A pain sliced through his chest. "I'm not your first mate." He hadn't really thought about that before. Brownie had said the scar came from a bar fight. Only mates could scar each other.

Brownie's eyes flashed dangerously as he finally focused on Yuri. Yuri recoiled a hair at the rage he saw in Brownie. "I'm not a fucking wolf."

Yuri swallowed. "Okay." Even he heard how small he sounded. Everyone was always angry with him. Brownie was the one person he didn't want to feel that way with.

Brownie swiped a hand over his face. He looked defeated. His eyes seemed almost sad as he straddled Yuri's body. While keeping his weight balanced on his knees and heels, Brownie effectively kept him pinned. "Please listen to me."

At the pleading in Brownie's voice, Yuri nodded. "Of course. Anything." He meant it. Yuri would always do anything Brownie needed.

Brownie's muscles relaxed. He obviously recognized Yuri's loyalty. Yuri would always give him anything. "I know I've said this all before, but I need you to really hear me. Hellhounds aren't part of your world. We aren't created or ruled by Odin. I'm not like you. My skin scars. I can talk in animal form and my blood would boil away anyone else's skin. Yet you drank it... like only a true mate could. We don't procreate. In fact, most creatures on this side of heaven never receive mates. It's almost unheard of unless we leave here to serve Celeste. My only guess is you're the one she blessed. Not me. I'm only benefiting from the grace she's extended to you."

Yuri clung to every word. He was fascinated and confused. His mate was a mystery to him in so many ways. Yuri realized how little he understood about the underworld.

Thankfully, Brownie kept talking. Yuri knew he wouldn't let Yuri live in the dark. "Hellhounds don't kiss or care about each other. We don't have parents. There's no such thing as nurturing. We exist to serve Lucifer. In our downtime, maybe we'll fuck, but that's also an act of bravery. It's vicious and dangerous, since we might choose to tear each other's throats out. This world is nothing like yours. Being with you, there's no way you can understand what that's like for me. You are softness and sunshine. Laughter and warmth. You're everything I never knew before you. There's nowhere else I'd rather be right now. There damn sure isn't another beast I want to touch." He motioned between them. "This is a blessing I couldn't even dare to dream. There's no one else, period. You're everything."

Yuri sniffed. He hated how close to tears he was. Life had been way too hard. Brownie felt way too much like Yuri had a new family.

"I'm your mate. I am your family."

The softly spoken words broke Yuri. He rolled upward, tossing the blanket aside, and snagged Brownie's neck, hauling him down. Yuri claimed Brownie's mouth, and all thought vanished. He was just a man beneath his other half. Yuri couldn't get close enough.

Brownie had gone from never kissing to unable to get enough in a single day. There was no way he could have known exactly how carnal the act could be. He was transfixed. Nothing existed but Yuri's mouth. He should have realized how amazing this would be simply by how desperate he always made Brownie to groom him. Brownie had never spent so much time licking every inch of anyone. He had never groomed anyone other than himself before Yuri. Why hadn't he immediately recognized Yuri as his mate? The way he had wanted to take care of him from minute one was unfathomable before him. This wolf was his.

Brownie desperately wanted to be inside Yuri. He was just as out of depth here as he had been with kissing. Brownie wanted every second to feel good to Yuri. He didn't want to hurt him. That wasn't something Brownie knew how to do. But he felt everything Yuri felt, so he hoped he would figure it out.

His mouth moved to Yuri's ear. He wanted to lick it. "I want to make love to you."

"Yes." The breathless whisper cut through Brownie's soul. The way Yuri gripped his arms and writhed beneath him said a lot about his restlessness. He wanted Brownie too. That still fucked with his head. Yuri was so flawless... except for Brownie's bite mark. Brownie's stomach growl. *His.* Yuri belonged to him.

"Hold on. Just give me a second." It really took some rooting for Brownie to find lube. He owned it, but—as he had told Yuri—his life was very different from Weres. The sexy way Yuri's whiskey-colored eyes watched his every move had Brownie near to panting. He wet his fingers and got to work, getting Yuri as wet as possible. Fuck. He was a man on the edge. Everything was so goddamn gorgeous about Yuri. They genuinely didn't match. He couldn't stop being blown away that Yuri even let him touch him. His hunger turned dangerous. He was used to claiming what he wanted. Brownie turned more treacherous by the second. The demon dog inside him was barely held at bay.

"I want you inside me."

Brownie swore he lost sight at Yuri's desperate-sounding words. A red haze coated his vision. He sounded demonic when he responded. "I'm barely me right now. Don't toy with me. The hellhound inside me wants to claim you."

In a show of strength, Yuri rolled upward, grabbed Brownie, and twisted. Brownie blinked at the ceiling. He didn't get taken down. His confusion lasted for less than a second when Yuri's tight body sank onto him. Brownie's back bowed as Yuri's heat squeezed his cock.

"Holy fuck, Yuri. I—" He had no idea what he meant to say. His brain flew out the window when Yuri lifted and lowered himself, taking Brownie even deeper. Everything short circuited. His claws tore through the sheets. He fought to keep them clear of Yuri's beautiful skin. The sounds he made were as unfamiliar as finding himself on his back.

Yuri's tongue circled Brownie's nipple.

Brownie realized he could slightly separate what he felt from what Yuri felt.

Damn. He wasn't in pain. Yuri wanted this every bit as badly. He used Brownie's body to take his pleasure. That was all he needed to know. It was also the last coherent thought he had. Yuri's fangs sank into Brownie's chest, right above the nipple he had just licked. His entire body reacted. The growl he released would have scared any other beast. He felt Yuri's pride, along with his pleasure. Brownie was no longer in control. His needs were. He flipped, pinning Yuri beneath him. Brownie tore into Yuri's throat and drank. A blinding light of ecstasy flashed through his mind. The sweet taste of Yuri's life-giving force brought Brownie slamming back down to reality. Yuri had already been lightheaded once tonight from blood loss.

Brownie quickly licked the wound, sealing it. Even as he watched the scar appear, his pride didn't outmatch his worry. "I'm sorry. Damn. I wasn't thinking. You have to make me stop before I do stupid shit. I'm so sorry."

Yuri's tongue filled his mouth, silencing him.

Brownie's heart slowed. His mind stilled. Peace and satisfaction settled on his shoulders. He had never experienced anything truly beautiful before. This had been soul-searing. He floated on a cloud. Brownie had felt pride and attachment. Being Lucifer's protector gave him that. Brownie had never felt this before. It was something new. Something he didn't know how to name. It was beautiful and ugly. Affec-

tion and jealousy. This was a deep pos-
sessiveness he would tear anyone and
anything apart to keep. If it had a name,
he didn't know it yet. All Brownie knew
was they were for eternity and nothing
could touch them.

A cold wind washed over Fen's skin. He
shifted in his sleep, searching for his
blankets. The air burst from his lungs
on a gasp before icy water filled them

just as quickly. All he saw was murky blue sea water in every direction. He tried swimming in what he hoped was the direction of the sky. His arms ached. He was too panicked to even question how he had ended up here.

Then Fen stared into a huge electric-blue eye. He was transfixed. Almost hypnotized. The eye shrank until it became the size of a human's. Frost-colored hair and perfect features accompanied the eye. There were two of them now. He stared at the most flawless man in existence.

A wicked-looking smile stretched the man's lips, as if he heard Fen's thoughts. Warmth engulfed him. He stood dry and firmly on the ground. His surroundings didn't matter. Only those blue eyes existed.

A finger trailed down his bare chest. "You smell like him. Why do you smell like him?" He leaned in close and took a long sniff of Fen's neck.

"Who are you?"

"I see. His mutt has a mate. You drank his blood. All his creations smell just like him. It makes sense his dog's mate would also carry his scent."

"Who are you?" Fen repeated the question a little louder. He hated being ignored.

Blue eyes snapped to his face again. "I should really stop wiping your memory. This constant reintroducing myself is tiresome. Unfortunately, I don't think you'd play the good little spy if I let you remember me. You may call me Monnie. Show me what you've seen." Monnie cupped his head.

Fen felt the guy trying to flip through his every thought, like reading a book. He fought him. Fen wasn't weak. He didn't know what the hell was happening, but he knew Yuri was his friend. He had offered his blood in a way most creatures would never. Fen couldn't let this being, or whatever he was, have his thoughts.

Monnie rolled his eyes and dropped his hands. "Another game we play each time I see you. We'll make a trade. Give me what I want, and you can have my blood."

A memory tried clawing at the back of Fen's mind. His inability to satisfy his hunger. It was this one. Whatever was in his blood was addictive. Fen wanted more every second of every day without knowing what it was he needed.

"Nae. I don't want your blood." Yuri had fed him. His powerful blood had helped. Fen didn't want to go back to craving something he couldn't have. Fen squared his shoulders and planted his feet, readying himself for whatever punishment would come. He was a warrior for a reason. Fen could take it.

Monnie invaded his space. His silky blue robe opened. A flawless body pressed against him. Fen's cock stirred. His body betrayed him. Monnie was sexual in a way Fen couldn't describe. Fen smelled the blood pumping through his veins. It smelled like sherbet ice cream and something else he couldn't describe. The desire and cravings were crippling him.

Then a sensation yanked at his gut—like getting hooked and reeled away.

"No!"

The vision of Monnie's enraged face disappeared. The cold water filled his lungs again, choking him. He watched the murky blue water zip past him. Finally, the warmth of his bed engulfed him. Fen shot upright. His gaze darted to every corner. He was completely dry. Fen shook his head. What a weird–ass dream. Everything had felt off since he had been abducted. Maybe he should ask Frost to take a look at him. Maybe there was something wrong. He knew next to nothing about any of the gods. Maybe they poisoned the skin the same way a demon did.

He settled back down and dragged more covers over him. There was a chill in the air. No wonder he had dreams about freezing. Fen shouldn't really need sleep, but he hadn't done much else in his off time for a while. As darkness tugged him under, a whisper brushed his mind. "Bring me the wolf."

Fen was asleep before he had time to grasp a word.

Chapter Four

BROWNIE COULDN'T RESIST LICKING his mark on Yuri's skin. Not only did he taste delicious, pride filled his chest each time he looked at it. He honestly couldn't believe this man was his. Brownie would never stop being awed.

Yuri stirred, making Brownie feel guilty. He tried to keep his voice low. "Don't wake up. I just didn't want to sneak away while you slept. I have to go watch Lucifer's back while he works."

"Mhmm. Okay." Yuri's eyes never opened. He simply swept his hand down Brownie's chest—like petting him.

A huge grin spread across Brownie's face. He adored Yuri. Brownie gave one last lick before slipping from bed. In hound form, he trotted down the hall and found Lucifer saying his goodbyes to Riku. He quietly waited until Lucifer joined him.

Lucifer patted his head before the two fell into step and headed for the torture rooms. "Nice mating mark you have there. I take it you found Yuri?"

"You could've told me instead of letting me make an ass of myself for months."

Lucifer made a humming sound—like he wasn't as sure. It helped a tad that he didn't seem to find humor in the situation. "Is that really what you think? Isn't it much better to tie yourself to someone you actually love? Who wants to feel duty-bound into an eternity of marriage?"

Love? He supposed there was a word for how he felt about Yuri after all. But he had felt something powerful from the first moment he saw Yuri, so he doubted it would have been duty that made him claim his mate. "Is that how you felt when you met Riku? Duty-bound?"

A loud bark of laughter burst from Lucifer. Blue eyes flashed his way, swimming with wicked humor. "I'm the fallen one. Duty doesn't mean shit to me. Greed is what I immediately felt."

Except that wasn't true at all. Lucifer forgot they had a mind connection. Brownie had been on Lucifer's emotional rollercoaster with him since he first felt Riku. That wasn't his only lie. Duty was what had them descending the stairs to torture the damned. Lucifer felt no pleasure at this chore. It was his responsibility. Brownie kept all that to himself, though. It didn't matter why Lucifer kept control as long as he did. The alternative was unthinkable.

"He's a good choice for you. You're too serious and he's a marshmallow. You'll be happy."

Brownie knew that. He already couldn't wait to get back to Yuri. Brownie hated the way he had left Yuri all warm and cuddly in bed alone. There wasn't an ounce of duty in the way he felt. In fact, he better understood the greed Lucifer mentioned. He couldn't get enough. Brownie equally understood Lucifer's emotional rollercoaster over Riku's initial rejection. If Yuri had rejected him, Brownie might have torn apart an entire demon village too to release some of the rage.

Lucifer ran his hand through Brownie's fur, making his eyes fall closed with affection. "Don't worry, my pet. I see no reason we can't keep things short today. There's nothing I'd rather be doing than Riku." A rumble of naughty-sounding laughter fell from Lucifer's lips. He sounded as evil as he could be. Lucifer opened the door to the torture room to complete pandemonium. Demons and the damned battled. They exchanged tired glances. It seemed they would be trapped at work longer than expected today. How tiresome.

Yuri wandered into the sitting room with his stomach growling. He felt the hum of Brownie at the back of his mind, but he didn't look too closely at his thoughts. Yuri had a feeling he didn't want to know what went on when Brownie worked. He was giddy as hell today, though. A night of sleeping in Brownie's arms had him floating on a cloud. He had a mate. Yuri wanted to skip like a little kid.

"There he is. I thought you planned to sleep all day."

Yuri smiled at Riku's greeting. "Hi. Sorry. I guess I was a little drained."

Riku's eyes flashed with humor. "I'll bet. Care to tell me about it?"

Yuri moved to join Riku on the couch. "It's nothing. I ran into Fen, and he's been having a hard time fully recovering since the whole thing with Jörmungandr, so I gave him my blood. It wiped me out more than I expected."

Riku playfully slapped his arm. "Not that. I meant that lovely new mating mark you're sporting."

Heat climbed Yuri's face. "Oh. That. So I guess I was pretty dumb for not realizing me being able to communicate with Brownie mentally meant he's my mate."

Riku made a helpless gesture. "I mean, you're the son of an alpha and a guardian wolf. He is an alpha. It wouldn't seem unusual for you two to speak mentally. I wouldn't have known in your place."

The comment gave him pause. Riku was a godling. "Did you know? About Brownie and me, I mean," he clarified.

Guilt passed over Riku's features. Yuri felt a shot of outrage before Riku immediately took it away. "Not at first, no. Lucifer had to tell me. I wanted to tell you, but he was afraid you two would claim each other out of duty and not love. It seems Brownie is pretty big on keeping his obligations."

That didn't surprise Yuri. His claim also planted a seed Yuri hated. Had Brownie claimed him out of a sense of duty?

"Let's go to town and grab you something to eat. I can feel your hunger and the guys won't be home for a while. It seems there was a bit of an uprising this morning."

Yuri's gaze snapped Riku's way. "Lucifer told you that?"

Riku was busy looking for his shoes. "Yeah. As soon as he walked through the door down there, it was all cursing and ranting." Riku flashed him a smile. "His thoughts are actually pretty hilarious. He has a very dry wit I adore."

Damn. He loved seeing Riku happy. Yuri hated the way he doubted everything now. Brownie hadn't told him anything about an uprising. His thoughts didn't bombard Yuri. "Yeah. I guess we should find something to do until they get home." He couldn't sit here with his thoughts. Yuri was too used to undermining himself with doubts.

"I let Lucifer know where we're headed. He'll probably tell Brownie, but you should let him know too, just in case. I'd hate for an enraged hellhound to storm the diner."

"Yeah." It also gave Yuri the excuse he needed to talk to him and soothe the ridiculous growing doubts that were drowning him. It wasn't Brownie's fault Yuri was like this. He focused on his other half. *Hey, sexy.*

Don't join me here!

The barked order had Yuri immediately withdrawing. He locked down his mind. "Let's go." Yuri suddenly had zero desire to be in Hell any longer. He wanted sunshine.

Chapter Five

IT FELT LIKE THE longest day of his life and he hadn't been gone that long. Brownie knew it was because he spent the day away from Yuri. He was more than a little irritated when not only could he not find Yuri, but Yuri had him totally locked out of his mind. The quiet was annoying. Plus, it made his chest ache when he couldn't immediately locate his other half. He was used to having that connection. Brownie hated to ask Lucifer and admit Yuri had him blocked, but desperation won.

"What happened to Riku and Yuri? I haven't seen either of them."

Lucifer didn't seem concerned. "Frost's place. They went out earlier for lunch and then Frost invited them to stay for a barbeque he's throwing this evening. I'm surprised Yuri didn't tell you."

Damn. Yuri had tried talking to him earlier. "He probably thought you'd pass along the information. Do you need me here?" He had to find his mate before he went insane.

Lucifer gestured with his head toward his bedroom. "Go. You can send my wayward mate home."

Brownie didn't need to be told twice. He was in Lucifer's room and through the mirror in under a minute. Brownie heard the laughter before he reached the backyard. A fire roared. Fen sat close to Yuri and Riku. All three were smiling and talking. Fen was way too close to Yuri for Brownie's liking. The cool night air had Yuri wrapped in a coat and scarf. It pissed Brownie off to see his mating mark was hidden. He maybe stormed the backyard a hair aggressively.

"Lucifer asked me to send his wayward mate home."

Riku and Yuri looked his way. No one seemed to notice his rage. Yuri's mind was still closed to him.

Riku chuckled. "Hey, Brownie. I was just about to head that way. Are you hungry?"

He was, actually. That took a backseat to his irritation.

"He is." Yuri tugged on his pants. "Come on. Sit. I'll fix you a plate."

Riku stroked his hair as he claimed the chair Riku vacated. He was used to being treated like a pet, no matter his form. Brownie belonged to Lucifer and by extension Riku. Plus, he loved being caressed, so he was unbothered. Before he had time to greet his mate properly, Yuri was on his feet and walking away. He supposed to make him a plate as he had offered, but fuck. Brownie was aggravated. It had been a terrible day. He just wanted his mate.

"Why do you look angry?"

Brownie glanced Fen's way at the question. He faked a smile. "I'm not angry. This is my face."

Fen shook his head and looked away. He didn't have time to question anything. Yuri returned with a plate and two beers. He kept one beer and sat. Yuri took a drink and didn't look Brownie's way. His irritation and fear spiked.

Why are you mad at me?

Even after the huge mental push to force his question on Yuri, Yuri didn't look his way. *Oh, am I allowed to speak to you now?*

Fuck. He had been in the middle of tearing a demon to pieces when Yuri reached out to him earlier. Brownie had panicked at the thought of Yuri seeing him like that. He hadn't meant to upset him. *You're always allowed. I'm your mate. Not your keeper. There are some places I don't want you to see. That torture room is one. Please don't shut me out.*

Yuri looked his way. Anger flashed in his eyes, but he kept their conversation private. *Oh. So you're allowed to shut me out, but you don't like it when I do it? Seems fair.*

Brownie swiped his hand over his eyes. He wasn't good at shit like this. Brownie loved Yuri. He didn't want him exposed to the evil of his world. Hell, he already felt like he robbed Yuri of the moonlight and trees. He honestly had no idea why Celeste had chosen him for this. Yuri had to think this was more a curse than a blessing.

"You love me?"

The quietly spoken question had Brownie meeting Yuri's gaze again. He looked blown away. Brownie hadn't thought to guard his thoughts. Not only was he not used to Yuri listening, Yuri had shut him out all day. That made it harder to acclimate to sharing his mind.

"You know I do. It's right there for you to see for yourself."

Yuri gave him a sharp nod. "Eat. Your hunger is gnawing at me."

Brownie shoveled food in his mouth. Honestly, he didn't taste a thing. Yuri hadn't returned the words, and he still kept Brownie mostly shut from his mind. He wished he was better. That was it. Just better. He knew he was a horrible mate. Brownie hadn't thought he would ever be one. It didn't surprise him at all that he sucked at it. He just wished Yuri didn't have to suffer because of his shortcomings.

Hey.

Brownie looked Yuri's way at the call.

Yuri smiled. *I love you too. Stop scowling at everyone.* The humor in Yuri's eyes had Brownie's shoulders relaxing.

"I missed you today."

Yuri's sweet smile was everything. "I missed you too."

Brownie nodded toward the beer Yuri held. "Drink your beer so we can go home." *I want you to myself.*

Yuri stood. "I'll say our goodbyes to Frost."

Brownie's hungry gaze followed Yuri. Yuri was right. Brownie was starved, but it wasn't for food. He had tasted something so much better. Now he couldn't get enough.

A young wolf Fen didn't know filled the seat beside him. He stared at the fire and ignored him. Fen assumed he simply took advantage of an empty chair. With Yuri and Brownie gone, there were two. The young one could bring a friend.

"He'll never notice you, you know? Not really. All Yuri sees is the hellhound. Don't ask me why. He's not very handsome and probably abusive."

Fen looked the guy's way with raised eyebrows. He half expected to find him talking to someone else. The guy stared at him. Fen glanced behind him, checking to see if there was any possibility the comments had been meant for anyone else. When he saw there was no other option than him, he met the bright yellow stare that still waited for his attention. "Who are you?"

Humor flashed across the guy's soft features as he held his hand out to shake. "Kyrie."

Fen shook. "Fen. Why would I want to catch the attention of a mated wolf?"

Something crossed Kyrie's features before disappearing behind a smooth mask. "Yuri isn't mated."

Fen nodded. "Aye, he is. That scary-looking hellhound is his mate. Of course, Yuri only has eyes for him. That's how it works."

"Ah. Well. I suppose that explains why he's never noticed me flirting."

Fen couldn't help but smile. Despite being rejected, Kyrie didn't seem upset. "To be fair, I think he's also the type to have nae idea when anyone is flirting."

"Part of his charm, really."

Bring me the wolf. A whisper on the wind caused chill bumps to rise on Fen's arms. Hunger scratched at his gut. "The moon seems extra bright tonight. I'm surprised you're not out for a run. Many of the Weres have already headed out."

Kyrie shrugged. "It gets boring going alone."

Fen stood. "Come on. I'll go with you. I'm nae a wolf, but I'm fast enough."

A bright smile lit Kyrie's face as he accepted the hand Fen offered. Something felt just within his reach, but he didn't know what.

A loud crash brought Fen's head whipping toward the sound. A huge guy Fen had never seen before looked embarrassed by the mess he had made, knocking over one of the many outdoor tables.

He winced. "Sorry. I didn't see that there."

"Can I help you?"

Fen went on alert at Frost's tone. He was here, on Frost's land, and was an unknown. He smelled like a bear. A Were. They had turned off the perimeter alarm since creatures would be coming and going all night. He should have stayed more vigilant.

"Um. Yeah. I think. I was told I would find..."

"Aspen?" Leif had one foot out the back door with a beer in hand. He stood frozen, staring at the new arrival like seeing a ghost.

The bear, who Fen assumed was Aspen, gave a small wave. He still looked uncomfortable as hell. "Hi. I was just asking for you."

Leif turned around and went back inside, closing the door behind him with a definite snap. Everyone exchanged glances. Aspen looked crestfallen on top of embarrassed.

"Oh no." Audor's whispered groan wasn't missed. It seemed he knew what this was about.

Discomfort was thick, he could taste it. Someone had to be the one to break it. Thankfully, the pack's leader, Waylon, was the first. As the town's alpha, that was his place.

"Would you like a beer?"

Kyrie stroked a hand down Fen's arm, bringing Fen's gaze back to him. "You should check on Leif. He's your brethren."

Damn. He hated that Kyrie was right, but Leif had looked devastated. "Raincheck on the run?"

Kyrie nodded. His bright yellow eyes swam with happiness. "Absolutely."

Fen would seek him out again, even though he didn't know why. There was just something about him. Fen had to find out what.

Yuri's entire body was ablaze. Brownie's rough tongue pulled at his skin, grooming him. He couldn't breathe. No matter how hard he sucked air, he couldn't think. Unlike before, Brownie intentionally tortured him. In the past, Brownie had done this out of affection and secret longing. Now that he had

Yuri, Yuri felt his evil satisfaction at knowing he drove Yuri insane.

You always have. I just don't care if I embarrass myself now.

Brownie shoved his tongue into Yuri's mouth, hungrily taking everything he wanted. So much delicious sweat covered Brownie's body, proving how hard he worked for Yuri.

Tell me you love me again or put me out of my misery.

Brownie lifted his head and held Yuri's stare, as if he needed Yuri to believe him. "I can do both. I love you." He rolled his hips, causing friction between their bodies with their hard cocks trapped between them.

A loud pant escaped Yuri. "I love you too."

Brownie rolled his hips again.

"Oh, Goddess."

Brownie didn't take mercy on him. "I love watching you fight to come." He heard the lid pop on the lube. "But I love watching you drip with my cum even more."

"Fuck." The breathless curse didn't even begin to cover how close he was to the edge. He genuinely thought his mind might snap. The combination of his lust and Brownie's made him insane. Then Brownie impaled him. It was over. His back bowed. A howl left his lips. Jets of cum hit his chest. The slight red tint to Brownie's eyes glowed brighter as he watched Yuri. Yuri felt the way his intense gaze never wavered.

"You can give me another."

Yuri was pretty sure he could not. In fact, he was seconds away from passing from this life.

Brownie kissed his neck and chuckled against his skin. "You're so dramatic. I promise you won't die." He thrust. "But you will blow for me again."

Yuri wanted to claim again that he wouldn't. But the moment Brownie began that rhythmic thrust, pressure built. He didn't know any longer if it was his or Brownie's orgasm that he felt growing. It didn't matter. Either way, Brownie was right. Yuri would blow again. When it hit, this time, Yuri couldn't draw a deep enough breath to make a sound. His orgasm mixed with Brownie's in his mind. Stars popped in his vision.

"You're the sexiest creature alive." Brownie whispered the words against Yuri's skin as he kissed his neck again. "I'll never let you forget it."

Brownie was the most loved creature in existence. Yuri would never let him forget that.

Chapter Six

THE BED SHIFTED SLIGHTLY, pulling Yuri from his sleep. He might have asked Brownie where he was going if he hadn't been so obviously sneaking around in the dark. Yuri watched him gather clothes and slip from the room. He gently prodded his mind and found Brownie had shut him out.

Yuri slipped from the bed and checked the hall. Finding it clear, he ran to his bedroom and threw on the first clothes he found—a tank top and jeans. He followed his mate's scent. When it led him outside, Yuri hesitated. He knew it wasn't safe without an escort. Once he left the protection of Lucifer's property, anything could happen to him. Curiosity beat him. He stayed close enough to Brownie to catch his scent, but stayed far enough back to keep Brownie from smelling him. He had the downwind advantage. Plus, Brownie had him locked out so tightly, there was no way Brownie would feel him following.

The scenery quickly changed from forest to city. It was almost jarring the way he went from being surrounded by trees to the streets of what could have easily been New York. Not that he had been there to know, but he had seen pictures. The only difference was the place was dead. Lights were mostly neon, leaving alleys dark. Trash blew across the streets and the stench of death hung in the air. The smell was almost choking and nearly cost Yuri his mate's scent. Luckily, he held on to it just enough to catch the final wisps of Brownie stepping through the door of what looked to be a biker bar. Yuri froze. Brownie had sneaked away to go to a bar. What the fuck? His heart raced so hard, his pulse pounded in his ears. If Brownie had wanted to go out, all he had to do was say so. Yuri wasn't holding him hostage. There was no reason to sneak around...unless there was a reason. He didn't know what to do. Anything could happen to him if he stepped inside. Brownie would definitely know Yuri had followed him. The place looked too small for him to hide. Fuck it. His mate would explain himself. Yuri was tired of being kept in the dark. Brownie could claim he didn't want Yuri to see the dark parts of his life all he wanted. But if those dark parts included him fucking with someone else, Yuri would tear Brownie's heart out and eat it while he watched.

He took a breath and opened the door. The place was packed with hellhounds and the scattered demon or two. He half expected the entire bar to fall silent at his appearance, but most averted their eyes as he passed. It was almost odd the way the crowd parted and immediately shied away. Yuri didn't have time to puzzle over it. His gaze went straight to the back of the bar where Brownie had his head together with someone else. The guy had glowing blue eyes. He was strangely beautiful and didn't fit the crowd at all. The way he smiled at Brownie had a low growl rumbling in Yuri's throat. He was too pissed off to be scared. Brownie stood way too close, which wouldn't have been a big deal if Brownie hadn't sneaked away to do it. The growl deepened and turned deadlier when the pair headed toward a nearby door. They stepped inside and closed the door behind them.

Yuri didn't stop to think. He didn't fear the things he likely should. Since he fully intended to kill two men, nothing much mattered any longer. He let the rage build. Yuri hadn't fought anyone since losing to the Wulfe alpha. This was different. He thought he had nothing to lose back then. Now it was actually true. If he had to suffer, these fuckers were going with him.

Yuri stormed across the bar. No one got in his way. No doubt he bled fury. Without a single thought, he lifted his foot and kicked the door in, taking it completely off the hinges. It didn't matter he didn't find what he expected. Blue Eyes sat on a desk while Brownie stood near the door. Yuri nearly took him out with his kick. The growl in his throat sounded in his voice as he fought the shift. "What in the fuck is this?" The wolf in him lunged with zero permission from Yuri. This one thought to seduce his mate. He would have to do it in several pieces.

Brownie snatched him from the air. "Stop, Yuri. Desir is a demon. You can't touch him without getting demon sickness."

Yuri didn't give a shit. He fought against Brownie's hold. Why did he have such a humongous mate? Fighting the vise around him did nothing to cool his temper. There would be nothing left of the demon when Yuri got through.

"You sneak away to meet someone else and expect me to give a fuck about any sickness?"

Humor flashed in Desir's eyes, obviously unaware of how close he was to serving eternity in shreds. "Ah. The mate I've heard so much about. Lucky bastard. All that fiery passion must be delicious. We should all be so blessed." He laughed. "Well, maybe not all of us. After all, it's Hell." He stood and circled the desk to claim the chair behind it. "Don't worry about the door. I have minions for that."

Brownie didn't respond. He carried a still struggling Yuri through the bar. Hellhounds bowed as they passed. If anyone found the situation funny, they didn't show it. When the stinky night air slapped him in the face again, the fight left Yuri. He went limp. The entire situation was typical of Yuri's life. He didn't know why he bothered to fight in the first place. There was no such thing as happiness for him. The pack should have torn him to pieces along with his parents. Maybe he would have found peace in the afterlife. Then again, he likely would have just ended up here anyhow. All he felt now was defeat.

Brownie stroked him—like he petted Yuri in wolf form. "It's okay, beautiful. You're right to be angry. But just listen for a second, okay?" He walked, carrying Yuri away from the city and diving back into the trees. Yuri didn't bother responding. The life had gone from him. He was tired. Brownie kissed his nape.

Yuri didn't look away from the ground. He stayed completely limp in Brownie's arms. Yuri understood now. He recalled the way Riku had simply gone to bed and given up when Lucifer had left him behind. That was what Yuri wanted. He craved crawling beneath the sheets and sleeping forever. There was nothing for him here.

Brownie held him tighter. "Stop. It's not what you think."

Those words spurred some hot embers to life in his chest. "It's never what anyone thinks, is it? Tale as old as time." Even he heard the venom in his voice.

"This time, it really isn't." Brownie sounded truly upset that Yuri wouldn't believe him. "Desir is my pipeline to Celeste."

Brownie's explanation was so wild, it actually broke through Yuri's rage. It was a very random thing to say. Too random to be a lie. "What?"

Brownie stopped and sat. He kept Yuri tucked in his hold, but rearranged his body so he would be more comfortable and could hold Brownie's stare. "Celeste can't see her brother here, but she loves him and misses him. The only way she can get updates about his health and safety is from a select few of us who pass the information along. I didn't tell you because I can't risk Lucifer finding out. Riku can't know. No one can know. Lucifer cares about me, but I don't know if that would stop him from killing me or tossing me to the demon horde if he knew. She chose me. It's a great honor to serve, but I never wanted you to be put in a place to choose."

Brownie's mind was open to him again. He saw the truth. There were memories of him with Celeste. He felt the way Celeste stroked his cheek and praised him, promising blessings. "You're my mate. There's no choice to be made."

A long, loud, and tired-sounding sigh rang out around them, turning Brownie's blood cold, and by extension, his.

Lucifer lightly dropped from the sky to stand over them. His long wings brushed the ground.

"Ugh. I can't take it. You two have been very tiresome these past months." He focused on Brownie. "Do you genuinely think a damn thing gets by me?" His eerie light blue gaze shifted to Yuri. "Do you honestly think hellhounds are blessed with mates? My sister never gives mates to any of my creations without them working for her. That's how she so easily gets people to betray me."

He felt the way Brownie searched for something to say. His shoulders fell. It was obvious Brownie never meant to betray Lucifer. He didn't see it that way at all. Love had driven him to ensure Celeste knew Lucifer was safe.

She couldn't help him if she couldn't see him. It was extra protection Lucifer needed. She was his twin. Lucifer mattered to her.

Lucifer focused on Brownie again. "I know." He sounded soft in a way Yuri had only heard with Riku.

Yuri didn't know if Lucifer commented on the same thoughts he heard or if they held a secret conversation.

Lucifer's tone turned stern. "Where are you supposed to be right now?"

Brownie didn't hesitate. "At home, in bed with my mate."

"Exactly," Lucifer said, sounding annoyed.

"Where am I supposed to be?"

"In bed with your mate." This time, there was a bit of humor in Brownie's answer. Relief poured through Yuri. Brownie and Lucifer could speak telepathically. That meant Brownie saw a side of Lucifer only Riku did. If he relaxed, that meant Yuri could too.

"Damn right. Now, I shouldn't have to climb my ass from bed and fly all over Hell to keep your mate safe because you're sneaking away. You're lucky he didn't rip Desir to pieces and eat your heart. It would've been within his rights to do so."

"I know." Brownie sounded so calm and sure—like he believed Yuri could do those things if tested.

"Don't pull this shit again."

"I won't."

Yuri heard the truth in Brownie's voice and felt his pride in serving Lucifer. It fully hit him. Celeste had blessed him with an amazing mate. He hadn't really slowed down and let reality sink in. Now that it had, he was nearly moved to tears. Surely she didn't see him as his father's son if she gave him such a great partner to share forever with. His throat swelled.

Brownie stood. He still didn't set Yuri on his feet, which was good, since he didn't think he could stand. Life had really been a rollercoaster for a while now. He just wanted to rest and be held.

I've got you.

The sweet words caressed his brain and warmed his skin. Lucifer took to the sky—like a rocket. Yuri rested his head against Brownie's chest and listened to his heart beating. That was his. He couldn't believe it.

Brownie's pulse beat in his ears. He could barely breathe. First, that door exploded beneath Yuri's fury. If he hadn't been fast enough, Brownie would be begging Lucifer to take away Yuri's demon sickness right now. He had barely recovered from Yuri's fury before Lucifer had been there, forcing Brownie to face the reality of Lucifer knowing about his meetings with Celeste all along. Fuck. He could barely think. Everything about the night could have gone so differently. The collar around his neck felt heavier than usual. He wasn't so sure he deserved it. Lucifer had trusted him. Maybe he wasn't a good guardian after all. He obviously wasn't a good mate either. It seemed everyone he cared about deserved better than him.

"Your thoughts are hurting my chest. I'm so fucking embarrassed about the way I handled things. When things go wrong, I really just default to fighting."

Brownie carried Yuri inside and headed straight for their bedroom. He didn't respond until he set Yuri on the bed and worked to remove his shoes. "Of course you do. Anyone who has ever been made to feel powerless understands that. All it takes is one time of feeling like you should've fought to make you choose that option for the rest of your life." He stole Yuri's shirt because he loved Yuri's body, and it should never be covered. "Plus, you weren't wrong. If the shoe had been on the other foot, there would've been a bloodbath. As Lucifer said, it was your right."

Yuri cupped his face and stopped him, forcing Brownie to focus on him rather than his hands. "Maybe, but that's not who I want to be with us. I am so, so blessed to have been given you. All I want is to peacefully savor that."

Brownie turned his head and pressed his lips to Yuri's wrist. He dragged his scent into his lungs. Brownie loved him so fucking much. He didn't want to fail at being his mate.

"You're not."

Brownie automatically met Yuri's stare at the love that sounded in his voice. His chest swelled at the sight of that same love staring back at him.

"We're learning together. The two of us walked into this blind. I've never known a loving home, and you had to fight your way into one." Yuri made a helpless gesture. "At least we're fighting to keep each other. That says a lot, I think. That's definitely the type of mate I prayed to have."

"Me too." If it had been anyone else, Brownie would have been horrified to admit he prayed for anything, especially when no one heard him here. But it was Yuri, and he wanted Yuri to see all of him.

Yuri placed a sweet kiss on Brownie's lips. It did something to his chest he liked. He didn't know how he had gone from being the most feared hellhound to needing this affection to survive. Brownie had no complaints. He nuzzled Yuri, marking him with his scent. Brownie couldn't help it. The move was instinctual.

"You're still the most feared hellhound. I'm sure if I wasn't your mate, I would've been eaten alive when I walked into that club. I saw the way they bowed to you."

"It's only because Lucifer watched. If I hadn't been so terrified of you, I would've felt him too." He tumbled Yuri backward and crawled on top of him.

Yuri laughed. "Okay. You weren't scared of me."

Brownie couldn't stop smiling, even as he tried to speak and steal kisses at the same time. "Of course I was. You should've seen you. That's why no one dared to touch you. There's no one more terrifying than a scorned mate. No one would've dared step in your way. You kicked through that door like a true badass."

Yuri's body shook with laughter. He covered his face with both hands. Brownie felt the embarrassment rolling off him in waves. "I can't believe I did that."

"It was sexy." Brownie kissed his neck. He never got enough of tasting his mate. "You make me proud as hell."

Yuri dropped his hands, but he still looked horrified.

Brownie refused to let him be embarrassed about loving him so much he would enter a bar filled with hellhounds to kick in a demon's door. He never dared to hope he would have this kind of love. Brownie wanted it with every fiber of his being.

Yuri buried his fingers in Brownie's hair. His breathing turned ragged as

Brownie enjoyed licking his chest. "I love you so fucking much."

A possessive growl vibrated in Brownie's throat. "Mine." He licked Yuri's nipple. "All mine." His hands ran down Yuri's body, shredding Yuri's jeans along the way.

Yuri shook with laughter. "Ah, man. These are the jeans I just bought."

"I'll take you shopping tomorrow."

"It's okay. You're worth losing my clothes." Yuri's claim sounded breathless. "In fact, there are definitely too many clothes between us right now."

At Yuri's claim, Brownie raced to have them both nude. He didn't feel right until their bare skin molded. His heart sighed. Fuck. How had he survived before this? He couldn't stop his tongue from stroking every place he could reach. In no time, he had Yuri's cock in his mouth. He was so delicious.

"I want to do the same. I need to taste you too."

The moment the words died on Yuri's lips, Brownie rearranged their bodies so Yuri could suck him too. His eyes tried rolling back in head at the first lick. This was definitely something hell-hounds never allowed anyone to do. It was way too dangerous and vulnerable of a position to be in. Everything about them was different from anything he had ever known before. It was Yuri. It was his mate. No one was trusted more. There was nothing he wouldn't give him or try for him. He was pretty sure he would die soon, though. Yuri's mouth felt amazing on his cock. He didn't even think about what he did. Brownie simply licked and sucked with his entire focus locked on everything Yuri did. The closer he got to the edge, the more he gave. He needed Yuri's orgasm. When Yuri blew, Brownie did too. He saw rainbows of color as Yuri took him to another universe.

"Damn. I love you." The breathless words were all Brownie could muster. He knew to the depths of his soul that he would have a beautiful life with Yuri. Brownie couldn't be more thankful.

Chapter Seven

ANYONE WHO THOUGHT A forest was quiet had never been in a forest. Nature was loud as hell. The stars were beautiful, though, and the sounds were way more peaceful than the horns and sirens of the city. Frost loved that he could look at the stars and see them so clearly. Now that he knew the heavens truly existed, the sky was twice as magical. It didn't hurt that he used an extremely sexy chest as a pillow. He twirled one lock of Gemini's long blond curls around his finger. Frost hadn't felt this at peace in a long time.

"I can't believe how quiet things are tonight."

A groan burst from Frost. "Never say that. In the emergency room, that's always when things go to hell."

Loud howls rent the air, making them laugh at the timing.

Gemini ran his hand down Frost's bare torso. "I guess there goes the silence."

"Honestly, I expected more animal sounds tonight. Usually, the frogs are loud as hell. It seems like we either chose a good spot, or not, considering not as many pack members are joining the full moon run tonight, but we can still hear them."

Gemini made a humming sound. "I still doubt we'll see any of them. They can smell us. They'll stick to where they have privacy too." As if the universe had to make a liar of him, two beasts burst through the trees before disappearing again into the brush. "I can't believe Yuri convinced a hellhound to join the run. They are notoriously anti-social." Gemini paused for a second. "And violent."

"You don't think Yuri is in danger, do you? He's so young."

He felt Gemini shrug. "They're living with Riku. I think he'd tear the hound apart before he let him hurt Yuri."

"True." Frost didn't know enough about hellhounds to form an opinion. "I love this. We don't get enough of this peace."

Gemini toyed with Frost's nipple, as if it was an absent-minded motion. "I don't care. Well, I do. I know how that sounded. What I meant is, I don't care how few and far between these moments are. I'd rather have this with you than anyone. I'd rather be right here, holding you, than be anywhere else in the universe."

A smile tugged at Frost's lips. As much as it irritated him to admit, Lucifer's interference had helped quite a bit. Months back, he had sent a demon to take over Frost's job at the hospital so Frost could focus on doing only home health care. By extension, the move gave him way more time with Gemini. He couldn't explain why he felt such an attachment to Lucifer. He was supposed to be the most hated being in existence. Yet he didn't deserve it, and Frost knew it. He couldn't unlearn that fact. Plus, Frost was here with his mate and not working himself into the ground. That was the second greatest gift anyone had ever given him after Gemini.

"I love you." Frost couldn't resist saying the words. He adored everything about the mate he had been blessed with.

"That's good to know, since I worship the ground you walk on."

Frost smiled so hard, his face hurt. Their fingers linked. When they did, Frost's hand glowed. "Yeah. I'm just going to pretend I didn't even see that."

Gemini brought Frost's hand to his mouth and kissed it. "You're special. It's okay to embrace it. I'm proud as hell of you."

Frost appreciated the sentiment, but he was terrified of what he might become if he fully embraced whatever was happening to him. He knew he should ask questions. Frost should want to know more about this gift that supposedly lived in his blood, but he didn't. All he wanted was this: a perfect night beneath the stars with his mate. Everything else could wait. He kind of wished it would wait forever. Frost wasn't so sure he wanted this curse.

Yuri snuggled deeper into Brownie's hold. The moonlight washed over his skin, making him feel alive. Every night with his mate was like living in a dream. Still, Yuri hated to keep Brownie somewhere where he obviously felt the need to be on guard the entire time. Guilt already ate at him.

"I guess we should get home before everyone comes stumbling from the woods, nude and holding their shoes like sneaking home after a drunken night out."

He felt more than heard Brownie laugh. His tongue swiped the shell of Yuri's ear. "We can wait a little longer. I feel your happiness. You shouldn't always be cooped up in Hell. I'm cool."

Yuri shrugged. "It's okay if we go home. I could put on that leather outfit you just bought me, and you can take me for a spin on your Harley. You could try to concentrate while I risk death, trying to seduce you."

"That is a nice picture you're painting, but your suggestion has you putting on clothes." His hand smoothed over Yuri's bare stomach. "I much prefer you nude. You can seduce me here."

"You could always take me for a ride nude. That would turn some heads."

Brownie's laughter deepened, making Yuri's face hurt from smiling. He had never been more in love with life. Every day, he understood more about how blessed he truly was. This was literally a match made in heaven.

The brush shook. Yuri sniffed the air. He didn't bother moving. It was only Waylon. He imagined the guy intentionally made noise to keep from startling them. A surprised hellhound wasn't a good thing. Finally, Waylon stepped from the trees in wolf form. He had his vampire mate with him. Waylon turned human. "Hey, guys. I'm glad to see you out with us tonight."

Iridescent blue vampire eyes caught the moonlight and reflected it as he stared at Yuri. He had every right to hate Yuri for attacking his mate, but there was no animosity in his eyes.

"Yuri twisted my fingers until I agreed."

Yuri playfully smacked Brownie's stomach at the claim. "I'll twist something for sure if you keep talking shit."

Audor chuckled at the threat.

Waylon stayed professional, as always. "When do you plan to join the pack, Brownie?"

Brownie snorted.

Waylon smiled. "Yeah, I know. But I also want you to know you're welcome anytime. Everyone enjoys having you around."

Yuri felt the way Waylon's claim moved Brownie. His respect for Waylon doubled. The guy was definitely alpha material. Not like his dad, but a genuine leader. This town was lucky to have him.

Howls cut through the darkness.

Waylon's chin lifted as he sniffed the air. He flashed them a smile. "We had best get back to it while there's still time." He was a wolf again in an instant.

"See you."

Audor winked as he passed, following in his mate's wake.

Brownie waited to speak until they were alone again. "This is such a hodgepodge group. I've lived a long time, and only recently have I seen different species set up communities together. It's happening more and more often. Power in numbers, I suppose."

Brownie's claim of living for a long time gave him pause. Since they basically lived forever, most creatures never thought much about age. It occurred to him he hadn't asked about Brownie's. "How old are you, anyhow?"

He felt Brownie shrug. "I was spoken into existence too long ago to recall."

That was fascinating. "Lucifer just speaks his creations into existence?" He knew Brownie had said once that hell-hounds were created by Lucifer's hand.

Yuri had just assumed he meant in the same way Odin created wolves. He had never heard of anything being spoken into existence.

"Of course," Brownie answered, as if that should have been obvious. "He cannot allow reproduction among his creations. There is no such thing as births or procreation in Hell."

The possibilities his words opened were endless. "So, technically, he could just speak a child into existence for Riku and himself? Damn. That would be a beautiful baby."

He felt Brownie hesitate. "I never thought about it, but I suppose he could."

They were both silent, as if neither wanted to be the one to state the obvious. Brownie broke first.

"I suppose he could also do the same for us."

A smile exploded across Yuri's face. He didn't know if he was a good choice to be a parent or if he even wanted that, but he loved the idea of a child half Brownie and half him. "They would be the most gorgeous child ever made."

Brownie tucked Yuri tighter into his hold and kissed his temple. "They really would be."

Yuri didn't know what he would want in the future, but he knew Brownie would be there. That thought alone made him happy enough to light three suns. Maybe they would circle back around to this conversation one day, or maybe this one time was enough. Either way, Yuri had the greatest of mates. He would never take that for granted.

Keep an eye out for the next Devilish, *Unwanted.*

About the Author

CHARITY PARKERSON IS AN award-winning and multi-published author with several companies. Born with no filter from her brain to her mouth, she decided to take this odd quirk and insert it in her characters. One of her greatest loves is writing morally gray characters. You'll find them scattered throughout her hundreds of titles.

*Nine-time Readers' Favorite Award Winner

*2015 Passionate Plume Award Finalist

*2013 Reviewers' Choice Award Winner

*2012 ARRA Finalist for Favorite Paranormal Romance

*Five-time winner of The Mistress of the Darkpath

Connect with her online:

*Sign up for her newsletter: https://bit.ly/charityparkersonnewsletter

*Join her readers' group on Facebook: http://bit.ly/CharitysTribe

*Website: https://www.charityparkerson.com

*A list of her social media accounts and giveaways all in one place: http://hy.page/charityparkerson